THE CASE OF THE
PLOT TO PULL THE PLUG

Hodder
Children's
Books

A division of Hachette Children's Books

Special thanks to Lucy Courtenay
and Artful Doodlers

Copyright © 2008 Chorion Rights Limited, a Chorion company

First published in Great Britain in 2008 by Hodder Children's Books

2

A Catalogue record for this book is available from the British Library

ISBN 978 0 340 95979 4

Typeset in Weiss by Avon DataSet Ltd,
Bidford on Avon, Warwickshire

Printed in Great Britain by
Clays Ltd, St Ives plc

The paper and board used in this paperback by Hodder Children's
Books are natural recyclable products made from wood grown in
sustainable forests. The manufacturing processes conform to the
environmental regulations of the country of origin.

Hodder Children's Books
a division of Hachette Children's Books
338 Euston Road, London NW1 3BH
an Hachette Livre UK Company
www.hachette.co.uk

LOOK OUT FOR THE WHOLE SERIES!

Chapter One

It was a quiet, frozen evening. Everything was still, all sounds muffled by the perfect blanket of snow which lay on the ground like icing sugar on a cake. Outdoor lights cast a warm glow on the whiteness, sending long navy-blue shadows where they caught the trees and shrubs.

"RAAARGHH!"

Allie, Jo and Timmy the dog hurled themselves over a hedge and threw snowballs at their cousins Max and Dylan, who were standing behind the sturdy snow fort they had built in Jo's garden. Max and Dylan ducked below the battlements of their snow castle.

"You're wasting your time, girls!" Max shouted, pushing his floppy blond fringe out of his eyes. "You can't touch us in Castle Dylanmax."

"I don't want to touch you," Jo called, her dark face glowing with mischief. "I want to whap you with snowballs! Come out and fight fair!"

"Yeah!" said Allie. Trying to sound tough wasn't easy for a bubbly blond California girl, but Allie was doing her best. "And could you please hurry?" she added plaintively. "I'm very cold."

"Jo and Allie want us to fight fair," Dylan commented to Max. He took off his glasses and polished them before setting them on the end of his nose again. "Silly girls," he sighed. "Silly, silly girls."

Moving to the tennis-ball serving machine next to him – which happened to be loaded with snowballs – Dylan turned it on. The snowballs blitzed over the wall of the snow fort, peppering the girls and Timmy. They rushed to hide behind a tree near the garden shed.

"Remind me," Allie grumbled, wiping snow from her face. "This is fun, *why?*"

Jo grabbed a spade, a bicycle-tyre tube and some bits of timber that were standing beside the shed.

"Because revenge is a dish best served cold," she explained, hefting her weapons thoughtfully in her hands.

"Well, serve it up," Allie said. "I'm running out of heat wraps."

Tugging a packaged therapeutic heat wrap from her pocket, Allie opened it up and pressed it to her face with a groan of relief. "Ahhhhh," she mumbled through the wrap. "Sweet, sweet warmth . . . Rats, it's cooling off."

As Allie opened another wrap, Jo finished making a crude catapult from the spade, the tyre tube and the timber. Timmy used his big black, brown and white paws to load snow on to the spade, and Jo quickly packed it into an enormous ball. Then she dragged the catapult into position.

"Hey, Jo," Max sniggered, "nice catapult! Too bad you don't know how to aim!"

Jo calmly aimed her giant snowball and fired. The snowball sailed harmlessly over the boys' heads, slammed into the steep roof of the house and dislodged all the snow which had gathered there. The snow promptly avalanched on top of Max and Dylan, burying them completely.

"Maybe you can give me aiming lessons some time," Jo smirked as the boys wiped snow off themselves.

"No," said Dylan, shaking his head. "You seem to have it worked out."

Suddenly the lights snapped off. Everything went dark, save for the pale blue glimmer of the snow in the thin moonlight.

"Whoa," said Max. "Power failure – must be snow on the power lines. People will be stuck in lifts, if this town had any. Lifts, I mean, not people." He paused and brushed snow off his head. "Obviously there're people," he added. "I've seen 'em."

"How hard did that snow hit you on the head?" Dylan checked, staring at his cousin.

WHHHOOOO!

The sound of a train horn blasted through the air.

"Pretty hard," Max admitted to Dylan. "I hear a train horn over there—" He pointed west. "When I usually hear one at night—" He pointed east. "Over there."

A mile away from the cousins, a train was barrelling along the snowy, unlit track. In the cab, the train driver was frantically radioing for help.

"This is the driver of the nine-forty from Langford," he shouted into his radio. "The electronic switches failed! We're on the wrong track – we're going to crash! Hello?"

Several miles further on, a second train was also on the track. And it was heading straight for the first.

Chapter Two

WHHHOOOO! WHHHOOOO!

The train horn blasted again. It sounded more urgent than before.

"We've got a problem," said Jo, her head cocked to listen.

"You're telling me," Allie grumbled, stamping her feet. "I'm so cold, my tongue is frozen. True story."

"The train," said Jo. "It's the nine-forty passenger express coming from Langford – it's on the wrong track. It's going to hit the eight-fifteen freight diesel on the spur out of Wexley."

"Wow," said Dylan in an awed voice, before

adding under his breath, in a sing-song kind of way: "Train-Geek . . ."

"Dylan, we can make fun of Jo later," Max said, running for the side of the house where four snowboards were leaning against the wall. "We can't let those trains crash!"

The 9.40 from Langford was still speeding helplessly along the track. The engine driver pulled the emergency brake. The train wheels locked and sparks flew into the snowy air. When the engine stopped, the driver hopped out of the cab and hurried along the line to a hand-operated switch at a siding. But he couldn't budge it.

"Agggh!" cursed the driver. "Frozen stuck!"

The track was beginning to vibrate. The 8.15 freight train from Wexley was approaching.

The cousins whizzed down a snowy slope, weaving expertly in and out of the trees on their snowboards. Barking madly, Timmy followed. When they reached the bottom of the hill, they found a ravine blocking their way. Max steered his board towards a fallen, snow-covered tree near the ravine edge, and used it as a launch ramp. The others followed, twisting their boards in mid-air to arrive safely on the far side. It was a desperate race against time!

The tracks were starting to rattle at the approach of the 8.15 freight train. The hapless driver of the 9.40 from Langford was still wrestling with the switch on the siding when Dylan screeched to a halt beside him, sending up a plume of powdered snow.

"Need a hand, Mister?" Dylan panted. "We've got eight of 'em."

Max, Allie and Jo arrived. They jumped off their boards and ran to help the driver apply more pressure to the frozen switch. The air was filled with the smell of diesel as the freight train rumbled towards them, blowing its horn and applying its brakes in a wail of steel.

SSSCCCCCRRREEEECHHH!

Timmy hurled himself against the switch – and in the nick of time, his added weight unstuck the handle and sent the freight train thundering harmlessly into the siding.

"Eight hands and four paws," Jo panted, taking

her hands off the switch. "Never forget the four paws."

The train driver looked green-faced. "Thanks, kids," he stammered. "I'll be blowed if I know why the back-up electric systems didn't work. I'm going to check me generator." He paused, and turned a little greener. "On second thought," he muttered, "I believe I'll throw up first. Excuse me . . ."

"If the switching system failed, this power cut wasn't just caused by snow on the power lines," Dylan said as the engine driver hurried away. "The whole sub-station must have overloaded and gone off-line."

"Wow," Jo said, opening her eyes comically wide before adding, in an imitation of Dylan's earlier sing-song remark: "Techie-Geek . . ."

"Could we discuss this over a cup of hot chocolate?" Allie asked, shivering as Jo and Dylan pulled faces at each other. "Or better yet, sitting in a tub full of it?"

Chapter Three

Somewhere outside Falcongate, a shifty-looking man in his mid thirties was sitting in a home office, surrounded by wires, banks of monitors and computer hard-drives. The room had a rustic, log-cabin feel to it with stuffed animal heads hanging on the walls. The air was filled with the humming, beeping sound of high-powered electronic equipment.

The shifty-looking man flipped a switch on his kettle and made himself a cup of hot chocolate. Then he switched on one of his computers and addressed a webcam.

"Nicholas?" he grunted at the webcam. "It's

Uncle Danny. You there?"

On his screen, a grainy webcam image appeared. It showed a nerdily-dressed thirteen-year-old, with floppy dark hair and glasses. He was munching on something.

"Hy'm beehr Umpo Hammy," Nicholas mumbled, his mouth still full.

"Swallow the apple," said Danny impatiently. "I can't understand you."

Nicholas held up an onion to the webcam. "'Tis an onion, fine sir," he said, in a drawling voice. "My favourite." He burst out laughing, a weird honking sound that filled Danny's home office.

"Strange boy, that," Danny muttered, turning away from the screen for a moment so that his nephew couldn't see him. Swinging back, he said: "Nick, the experiment was a great success. Falcongate sub-station shut down. Surging the power blew out the back-up systems as well."

"I knew it would," Nicholas bragged. "I'm the greatest hacker there is. I knew I could do it. I knew it I knew it I knew it I knew it I knew it—"

"Stop that," Danny ordered. "Now that we know you can hack into a sub-station, I've got another little job for you . . ."

Nicholas put down his onion, looking uneasy. "I dunno, Uncle Danny," he said. "It's not really legal. I bet they don't have onions in prison, you know what I mean, ha, ha, ha!" His honking laughter filled Danny's office again, making the older man wince. "Or, I don't know," Nicholas said, as if something serious had struck him. "Maybe they do."

Danny kicked back from his desk and linked his hands behind his head. "I dunno, Nick," he said craftily, staring at the ceiling. "Maybe you couldn't pull it off, anyway."

Nicholas leaned in to the webcam. "I can pull anything off," he said immediately. "I told you – I'm the greatest."

Danny smirked to himself. Addressing the camera again, he said: "OK, prove it. Meet me in Falcongate tomorrow and we'll see how good you are . . ."

He shut off his webcam.

"I'm melting," Nicholas shouted as his image dissolved and pixillated on Danny's screen. "I'm melting . . . ha, ha, ha!"

At Falcongate police station the following day, the Five waited politely while Constable Stubblefield struggled with an enormous, tough-looking villain who was clearly resisting arrest.

"Constable Stubblefield," Jo began as the policewoman efficiently spreadeagled the villain against her desk. "Could we talk to you when you're done with the big, scary guy?"

"Gladly, young Kirrins," Constable Stubblefield said, briskly frisking the villain and pulling various sets of car keys from his pockets. "I've nearly sorted out 'Car Thief' Herlihy."

"You've got the wrong bloke, I tell you," complained 'Car Thief' Herlihy. "I've never— Hee-hee! No. That tickles! No. Hee-hee . . ."

"You know that power failure last night?" Max said, as the car thief wrestled helplessly with the constable. "The Big Blackout?"

"Yes," said Constable Stubblefield at once. "My telly went off in the middle of the reality show where you marry a Prince. I do hope he picks that sweet, dainty Penelope." She paused and smiled a little dreamily, the heel of her hand still firmly planted in the small of 'Car Thief' Herlihy's back. "She reminds me of me."

"Sure," said Allie, trying to be nice as Dylan gave a startled cough. "Because you and that Penelope have the same . . . er . . . desk accessories."

Constable Stubblefield flipped the car thief on to his back. "All the critical systems in the county were out," she said. "Even the hospital."

"Hee-hee!" wailed 'Car Thief' Herlihy. "Not me arm pits! I can't stand it!"

"And you don't find anything strange about

14

emergency systems conking out?" Jo persisted.

"I'll tell you what I find strange," Constable Stubblefield mused. "That that loud-mouthed Veronica could get to the Final Round. She doesn't understand the Prince like Penelope and I do."

There was an uncomfortable beat.

"Do you find it strange that this gentleman has six sets of car keys on him?" said Dylan, breaking the silence.

"I, uh, park cars for a living?" offered the car thief hopefully.

Five minutes later, after Constable Stubblefield had dragged the protesting 'Car Thief' Herlihy into one of the cells, the Five left the police station.

"Good news, Allie," Jo joked, stamping her feet on the snow-coated steps. "It's getting colder!"

"I'm going to see if the computer shop has *Utopia 3*," Dylan decided. "You design a city where everyone lives in peace and harmony, then destroy it with flying wolves with laser vision. Pow! It's very educational."

"I can't take this freezing any more," Allie announced as Dylan sauntered away down the street. "I'm gonna get some cold-weather gear at Addington's. Unless I turn into an Allie-sicle first."

She started purposefully up the snowy street.

"Addington's is that way," Jo said, pointing in the opposite direction.

"Yeah," said Allie over her shoulder, "but the laundromat vent is this way. I've got my whole route planned out."

Jo, Max and Timmy watched as Allie scurried over to a nearby laundrette and warmed herself in the hot air from the dryer vents. Then she darted across the street to a Chinese restaurant and disappeared through the door. After a moment, she reappeared in the window, warming herself amidst a row of hanging, freshly barbecued ducks. Next on her route was a cart selling hot chestnuts, which she bought and then tipped down the neck of her sweater. Lastly Allie hurried into Addington's Outdoor Supply, where she again appeared in the window, unfolding blankets from a display and wrapping herself in them.

"Now I think about it," Max mused as the Addington's shopkeeper tried to take the blankets from Allie in an unseemly tug of war, "hot chestnuts sound pretty good . . ."

Dylan, meanwhile, headed for the door of his favourite place in the whole of Falcongate: Ye Olde Computer Shoppe.

"You're late, Nicholas," Danny growled, stepping up to Dylan from the shadows of the shop doorway. "We've got to get to my house and get you going on the computer."

Dylan blinked in confusion at Danny. "I'm sorry, do I know you? And what are you talking about?"

"No time for your jokes, Nick," Danny warned, his eyes darting left and right. "Here's an onion for the ride."

"Clearly I don't know you," Dylan said, taking the onion helplessly. "And I have no clue what you're talking about. *Hoimp!*"

Danny had grabbed his arm and thrust him into the back of a dark, powerful-looking car parked outside the computer shop. The large, roly-poly henchman at the wheel started the engine and roared away from the kerb, leaving Dylan looking out of the window, an alarmed expression on his face.

Chapter Four

Back at Addington's Outdoor Supply, Allie stepped out of the shop in a heavily padded snowsuit featuring a number of elaborate dials and gauges. Various electrical cords ran in and out of the snowsuit's sleeves, torso and legs. Allie pulled a thick instruction manual out of one of the snowsuit's many pockets, opened the first page and read:

" 'Engage Battery A by setting Thermostat B/C to Off/On. Press B. Invert B back to C.' "

"Have you been chosen to visit a space station?" Jo asked as Allie approached the chestnut stand where she, Max and Timmy were waiting.

"This thermal suit is wired for heat," Allie said, poring over her instruction manual. "But the instructions are impossible to understand, and the battery pack weighs a ton." She turned and pointed to a bulky battery unit built into the back of the suit.

"On the plus side," Max offered, "you're not turning into some hideous half-girl-half-robot, which is what I thought when I first saw you, so . . . yay!"

A big red car came down the street from the direction of Ye Old Computer Shoppe.

"And if Dylan's friend's car ever dies," Jo said, absently noting Dylan in the back seat with a roly-poly driver and a man in a dark beard sitting up front, "you can jump-start it."

Desperate to attract his cousins' attention, Dylan stuck his arm out of the car window and thumped his fist on the car door. Three rapid thumps, three slower ones, then three more rapid thumps.

Danny turned round from the front seat and glared at Dylan questioningly.

Dylan made a lame attempt at making beat-box noises. "Yeah," he improvised, pounding on the door again. "I got the hip-hop in me. Dawg."

"That's Morse code for SOS," Max said, staring as the car whizzed past.

"Tell me about it," Jo said, staring as well. "Dylan's in trouble!"

"And he's holding an onion!" Allie added in surprise.

Looking around for some means of transport, the kids spotted three dustbins in front of a house across the street. They quickly grabbed the lids off the bins and climbed aboard them like snow-saucers, with Timmy in Jo's lap. They started to ride down the sidewalk, quickly picking up speed.

A postman unwittingly stepped in front of them on the pavement. Timmy barked a warning, and the postman quickly stepped out of the way as the kids zoomed past.

"Good job, Timmy," said Jo, patting her dog as she slalomed along. "Signal, everybody!"

Tucking Timmy under one arm, Jo held out her hand to signal a right turn. Max and Allie did the same. They steered down an alley and emerged on to a snowy slope, which angled towards the road. Between the kids and the road was an outdoor horse enclosure, fenced in by metal bars. There was just enough space beneath the bottom bars for the kids to squeeze through, as long as they . . .

"Duck!" Max shouted.

The cousins leaned backwards. Passing safely under the bars, they headed straight for the occupant of the enclosure.

"Horse!" Allie yelled.

They all leaned backwards again, passing safely through the horse's legs.

"Duck!" Jo shouted again, as a startled duck started flapping away in front of them. "The noun, not the verb!" The duck gained a little height, forcing Jo to add: "*Now* the verb!"

They whizzed beneath the flapping duck and slid under the far side of the enclosure. The big red car was now in view below them, heading along the road.

They raced towards it, hoping to head off the car, but the car passed ahead of them in a spray of snow. Their dustbin lids hit the asphalt road and abruptly stopped, sending Jo, Timmy, Allie and Max flying through the air and into a snowbank.

"We have to work out where they're going," Max

spluttered, wiping snow off himself as the car zoomed out of sight, "and get Dylan back."

"Well," said Jo, "we know they're heading east."

Sparks began shooting out of Allie's snowsuit. "We also know my thermal suit can't handle a wipe-out," said Allie, starting to dance and hop around. "Unplug me! Unplug me!"

In the distance, the car headed away, carrying Dylan to its mysterious destination . . .

Chapter Five

Back in Falcongate, the cousins trooped back to the dustbins on the high street and disconsolately replaced the – more than slightly battered – dustbin lids. Allie, now wearing only jeans and a T-shirt, walked behind the others, shivering and slapping her arms to keep warm.

As they turned back to the street, a nerdy-looking lad of about thirteen approached them, tossing an onion up and down in his hand.

"Excuse me, fair maiden," said Nicholas, bowing to Jo. "Could you perchance offer information to a stranger in your bonnie burg?"

"Is there something wrong with you?" Jo

asked, perplexed.

"Cold . . . Cold . . ." Allie chattered behind Jo. "Think of hot things. Malibu in summer . . . Brad Pitt . . ."

"I crave the whereabouts of your local computer store," Nicholas continued pompously. "I'm thirty minutes tardy to meet my Uncle Danny." He waved his onion at Jo. "Care for an onion?"

"What's with all the onions?" Max demanded, as Allie began running in circles. "Dylan had an onion. What does your uncle look like?" he asked.

"Dark hair. Dark eyes. Dark beard," said Nicholas. "Dark. I'd say he's dark."

"The man with Dylan had a dark beard," said Jo thoughtfully, staring at the boy.

"Who is this Dylan you speak of, milady?" asked Nicholas, bowing to Jo again.

"If you don't talk normally," Jo warned, "I'm going to deck you."

"Ooh, feisty," grinned the boy. "I like that . . ."

"Dylan's our cousin," Max explained. He looked Nicholas up and down. "You look like him. Though you probably don't have the same birthmark he has – it looks like a circus clown buttering toast."

"Your uncle must have taken Dylan by mistake," said Jo.

"Could we move this conversation indoors?" Allie begged, still running round in circles. "'Cos now I'm cold *and* dizzy." She wobbled momentarily, then pitched over in the snow.

In a cosy pet shop round the corner, the timid shopkeeper, Mr Weatherwax, placed a parakeet carefully into an aviary full of other parakeets.

"There you go, Griffin," Mr Weatherwax crooned. "Nice and easy . . ."

The door of the pet shop burst open. Jo, Allie, Max, Timmy and Nicholas rushed inside, startling Mr Weatherwax before he could close the aviary door. Parakeets burst out of the open cage in a feathered cloud of colour.

"Oh, dear," Mr Weatherwax said helplessly. "The parakeets are rampaging again . . ."

"We'll help you catch them, Mr Weatherwax," Jo promised. "Just don't let any cats loose."

Everyone began leaping about after the parakeets.

"Do you know where your uncle is taking our

cousin?" Jo asked Nicholas, following a bird around the shop. "Answer normally," she added warningly.

Nicholas shook his head, ducking and bobbing to avoid the swooping parakeets. "I don't really know Uncle Danny very well," he said. "He had to go away, my parents said, for five to seven years."

"If you haven't seen him," Allie asked, retrieving a parakeet from a cash register drawer, "how do you know what he looks like?"

"Webcam," Nicholas explained. "He contacted me on the internet. He wanted to know if I could hack into this place's power station and shut it down. I knew I could. I knew it I knew it I—"

"You caused the power failure last night?" Max demanded. He snatched a parakeet out of a snake enclosure before it got eaten and popped it back into the cage.

"I feel awful about it, now," said Nicholas ruefully. "The news said it caused lots of trouble. That's my fault."

A formation of parakeets divebombed Nicholas. He flung his hands over his head. "Plus," he added, "now I'm getting attacked by parakeets and it hurts."

Timmy growled sharply at three parakeets.

Looking alarmed, the birds hopped back into their cage in a tidy line.

"What did your uncle want with you today?" Jo asked, helping Mr Weatherwax put one of the last birds back in the cage. "To help him download ringtones?"

"He said he had bigger plans, but he didn't say what," Nicholas explained.

"Bigger plans," Jo repeated grimly. "I don't like the sound of that . . ."

With a fluttering noise, the last parakeet settled on top of Jo's head and started preening. The others smirked.

"I look silly, don't I?" Jo said after a pause.

Back in Danny's rustic log-cabin, Danny and his accomplice Rufus led a blindfolded Dylan inside. They guided him to Danny's office, where the banks of computers blinked and hummed.

"Sorry about the blindfold, Nick," said Danny. "It's for your own good – you can't tell people how you got here if you didn't see how you got here." He patted Dylan forcefully on the head. "Your Uncle Danny cares about you."

"My 'Uncle Danny'?" Dylan repeated, catching on. "Right, my Uncle Danny. You're my Uncle Danny. Hiya, Uncle Danny."

Danny removed the blindfold. Blinking in the light, Dylan glanced around the room, taking in the many stuffed animals.

"Wow," Dylan said. "You must really hate animals." He started up from the chair and headed towards the door. "Well," he said cheerfully, "must be going . . ."

Danny laid a meatlike hand on Dylan's shoulder and steered him to the computer workstation. "You've got all the equipment you need, Nicholas," he said, pulling out the desk chair and pushing Dylan into it. "Do what you did last night, but with the Hartshire power station in the Midlands."

"Got it, Uncle Danny," Dylan said automatically, his eyes flicking left and right, looking for escape routes. "I'll get right on to that, Uncle Danny."

Danny was starting to look more relaxed. Dylan wasn't sure if he preferred him this way.

"I'll be back with all the stuff you love to snack on," Danny said genially, clapping Dylan on the back and heading out of the room with Rufus in tow. "Raw onions, raw anchovies, raw garlic, carrot juice . . ."

"I like that stuff?" Dylan muttered to himself, watching Danny and Rufus leave. "There's something very wrong with me."

He hunted around the desk. It didn't take him long to find a phone. Dialling quickly, Dylan listened and waited – and hoped that someone would answer.

Chapter Six

Mr Weatherwax was putting the last parakeet back into the aviary with an air of satisfaction. The others had flopped down on some nearby chairs, looking relieved. Allie meanwhile was busy removing an enormous rabbit from a cage and draping it round her neck.

"You're very cute," Allie informed the rabbit, patting its silky fur. "And, more important, warm."

Rinnnggg! Rinnggg!

The piercing sound of Allie's phone sent the birds scattering once more. Mr Weatherwax disconsolately set after them again, with Jo and Max's help.

"You're quite graceful when you chase birds," Nicholas offered, looking dreamily at Jo. "Like a ballet dancer-princess-angel-lady."

Jo swung round. "Let me explain something to you," she said. "Keep quiet."

"Hello?" Allie said breathlessly into her phone.

"Allie, it's me," said Dylan.

"It's Dylan!" Allie told the others in excitement. "I'm putting him on speaker."

Allie pressed a button as the rabbit round

her neck watched curiously. "Go ahead Dylan," she said.

Now the others could hear Dylan as well.

"I'm in a first-floor room, it's too far to jump," Dylan said. "Those guys who grabbed me think I'm some weird, bizarre freakazoid named Nicholas."

There was an awkward pause in the pet shop.

"Um," Allie said. "Nicholas is standing right here."

"Oh," Dylan said. "Does he look like he could beat me up?"

Allie glanced over at Nicholas, who tried to beef himself up a little.

"No," she said. Nicholas deflated.

"Great!" said Dylan, sounding relieved. "Anyway, they blindfolded me, but I smelled strawberries along the way, then we drove for another ten minutes or so. That Danny guy kept talking about 'seeing the ol' Squid Gang again'. And I'm going to have killer onion-breath for about a year."

There was a pause. Then:

"They're coming," Dylan hissed. "Got to go."

Dylan hung up just as Danny entered the office with a tray of food.

"Here are your favourite snacks, Nick," said Danny, setting the tray down beside the computer monitor. "Don't be shy – you'll need your energy."

Dylan eyed the food. He managed to down an anchovy, and took a bit of onion. "Mmmmmmmmm," he said feebly.

"Good boy," said Danny, lifting his hand and heading out of the room again. "I'll let you get to work."

As soon as he had gone, Dylan grabbed a yellow Post-it note. In desperation, he dabbed the sticky part on his tongue. But the onion and anchovy taste was there to stay.

"It's not strawberry-growing season," Max said to the others as Mr Weatherwax puffed his way round the shop for the second time.

"There's a strawberry jam factory on the B311," said Jo. "My school went on a field-trip there. The whole place was sticky. I'll bet Dylan's somewhere nearby."

"I'll help find him," Nicholas offered. "I don't like the way my uncle's been acting." He gazed goofily at Jo. "And I'll get to know this saucy

34

creature better," he added, making Jo shudder with distaste.

Over in the log-cabin, Danny's accomplice Rufus was watching a home video in the living room. On the screen, five thieves in masks were exiting a bank, carrying sacks of money.

"I remember that bank job," said Rufus, looking misty-eyed as the thieves piled into their getaway van. "That was my birthday. Happy, happy days."

The video cut to the thieves enjoying a picnic in the country, waving at the camera, playing games and doing silly dances.

"Hi, Squid Gang!" Rufus shouted tearfully at the screen. "Hi, Nobby! Hi, Stan! Hi, Porkpie! I miss you lads so much!"

"After Nicholas knocks out the power," Danny said, coming out of the office where he had left Dylan, "you can say hi to the old gang in person. When the juice goes down, the Squid Gang can just waltz out of prison."

Rufus frowned. "It might be better if they run," he suggested.

35

Danny looked at Rufus. "You're a hopeless idiot," he said.

Back in the computer room, Dylan was standing on a stack of chairs and removing a heating vent in the wall. He heaved himself up and crawled into the duct. Scampering triumphantly along the passageway, he made a turn, then another turn, pushed out another heating vent – and found himself back where he had started.

Hearing the door open, Dylan stopped sighing with frustration and scurried to the desk, where he quickly punched a computer key. He managed to bring up a screen displaying an assortment of system-status items as Danny entered.

"Uncle Danny!" said Dylan heartily, thinking on his feet. "Er, uh, I was just running diagnostics, making sure the system isn't infected. You don't want a sick system. Yuk!"

"No time for that," Danny said, coming closer. "In an hour, the lights have to go out all over England."

"But—" Dylan began.

Danny pointed an accusing finger at him. "Don't you go soft on me!"

"Oh! No!" Dylan said quickly. "Not soft! I'm tough! Gangster tough! Arrrrr!" He wrestled himself to the ground, and punched himself so hard that he managed to give himself a dead arm. "See?" he said feebly, trying to wiggle his fingers. "Tough."

Danny seized the phone. Dialling a number, he left the room with it.

"This day's turning out bad . . ." Dylan muttered, stopping the punching-act with some relief.

Chapter Seven

The bus trundled through the snowy countryside in the late afternoon light. Max and Jo rode together in one seat, each clutching a pair of skis. In another seat, Nicholas punched keys on his laptop. Timmy rode beside Allie, his head sticking out of the open window and his ears flying in the wind as he sniffed the air.

"Can we close Timmy's window?" Allie said through chattering teeth. "I'm turning into an ice-blended-mocha."

"He needs to be able to smell the jam factory," Jo explained.

Allie sighed and reached into her rucksack.

She began pulling on several layers of clothing: jumpers over blouses over sweatshirts over T-shirts over jumpers.

Timmy's nose twitched. He had smelled something.

"Woof!" he barked.

The cousins and Nicholas all turned to see a factory out of the window, adorned with a painting of the factory's cartoon mascot: a dapper-looking jam jar wearing a top-hat and monocle and carrying a walking-stick.

"There he is," Max said affectionately. "Jimmy the Jam Gent!" He considered something for a moment, before adding: "I don't know why jam would get all dressed up like that. I mean, sure, caviar would wear a top hat – it's fancy – but this is just jam."

The others waited. They were used to Max's rambling.

"Anyway," Max said, his eyes coming back into focus. "We should be about ten minutes from where they're holding Dylan prisoner."

"Speaking of prison," Jo told Max in a low voice as she glanced over at Nicholas. "When Field

Marshal von Geek over there said his uncle had to 'go away for five to seven years' – didn't that sound like a prison sentence to you?"

Max nodded. "I'll say. This Uncle Danny guy is bad news. Like when you're snowboarding, and you wipe out in yellow snow."

Jo drew back a little. "Thanks for that image," she said, looking revolted. "Nicholas," she called over the seat, "we really need to contact Dylan. Any luck finding a wi-fi hotspot?"

"Working on it, sweetums," Nicholas said in what he supposed was a seductive voice.

Irritated, Jo rose from her seat with her fists at the ready. Max restrained her just in time.

"That village down there should have an access point," Nicholas continued, pointing to a tiny village at the bottom of the hillside down which the bus was travelling. "Allie, could you hand me my computer bag?"

Everyone looked at the enormous ball of clothes, scarves, hats and mittens sitting in Allie's seat.

"I don't think I can even move," Allie said in a muffled voice from somewhere in the middle of the clothes ball.

Allie wiggled, overbalanced, fell out of her seat and landed on her back in the aisle of the bus with her arms and legs in the air, looking like an overdressed turtle in a touch of trouble.

In Danny's office, a stuffed grouse sitting on a plinth bearing a small plaque reading *'Tamed' by Daniel Ferguson* gazed down morosely at Dylan as he pulled up the *crimetoday* webpage on the monitor.

"Danny Ferguson," he read, "leader of the notorious Squid Gang, wanted for robbery and blackmail. Also plays bass in a 'Beatlemania' tribute band."

He scrolled down photos of Danny and clicked them to enlarge several mug shots: a surveillance camera shot of Danny in a bank; another of Danny playing bass wearing a wig and Sergeant Pepper outfit.

"Ferguson escaped from prison six months ago and is considered extremely dangerous . . ." Dylan continued. He faltered and stopped. "This has got to be a bad dream," he muttered to himself. Glancing around, he seized on a glass of liquid and tossed it in his face to wake himself up. The orange gunk oozed down his nose, round his chin and dripped on to his T-shirt. Sticking out his tongue, Dylan took a cautious lick.

"Nope," he said in disappointment. "Carrot juice. Yuk."

"It's getting dark, Nicholas," said Danny, coming abruptly into the office and approaching the computer screen as Dylan wiped up the juice. "Time to see what you've done."

Panicked, Dylan tried to block the screen with his body. "Before I show you," he said, stalling desperately for time, "let's see how many Plantagenet kings we can name."

"Enough of that, Nick," Danny growled, elbowing Dylan roughly aside.

The *crimetoday* webpage blinked out. It was replaced by a complicated diagram showing the electrical circuits of a power station.

"Good," said Danny approvingly. "You hacked into the system."

Dylan glanced thunderstruck at the screen. "I who'd into the *what?*" he stammered.

Chapter Eight

"I'm in," said Nicholas, tapping at his laptop as the bus trundled on down the snowy road. "I've sent a mirror program to Uncle Danny's computer. It'll look like your cousin knows what he's doing."

"Make sure it's safe for him to talk," Max said, looking at the screen over Nicholas's shoulder. "Send him this message – dot dot, dot dot dot, dot dot dash—"

"And add a smiley-face emoticon," Allie advised, still struggling on her back in the bus aisle. "People always like that. Whoa!"

The bus headed sharply uphill, sending Allie

43

rolling backward down the aisle almost as far as the driver.

Dylan gazed at the Morse code message on his screen. *Is it safe to talk?*

"I'll leave you alone to finish up, Nick," said Danny. "Don't let me down."

Dylan waited until Danny had left the room. Then he turned back to the computer. *It's safe*, he typed.

A webcam image opened up on Dylan's screen, showing Nicholas grinning goofily on the bus.

"Allow me to introduce myself," said Nicholas. "I'm Ferguson, Nicholas Ferguson. Ha! Ha! Ha! That's my James Bond," he added, by way of unnecessary explanation.

"Dylan!" said Jo, as she, Max and Allie crowded into shot behind Nicholas. "Are you all right?"

"Other than burping anchovy, I'm fine," said Dylan happily. "What's that big pile of clothes?"

"That's Allie," Max explained.

The pile of clothes waved. "Hi!"

"Wow," Dylan said, leaning in closer to the monitor. "She's put on weight since this morning.

Listen, this guy Danny Ferguson is a crook – he wants me to cause a power failure all over England."

"Actually," Jo explained, "he wants Nicholas to do it." She gazed sternly at Nicholas. "And you're not going to, right, Nicholas?"

"No, ma'am," Nicholas said, sounding meek.

Still addressing Nicholas, Jo said: "If your uncle wants to black out the whole country, wouldn't it have to be some sort of domino effect from a single station?" As Nicholas gathered himself for a suave reply, she warned: "Please answer without sweet-talk."

"Yes, that's how it would work, Sugarplum," Nicholas replied cheekily. Then his bottom lip puckered. "Stupid Uncle Danny," he muttered, "trying to trick me . . ."

Gathering himself, Nicholas focused back on the webcam. "Don't worry, Dylan," he said. "I can handle everything from my laptop. Just pretend you're working your system. Any questions?"

"Just one," Dylan said. "Why couldn't your favourite snack be ice cream?"

Max glanced at his watch. "It's been about ten minutes since we saw Jimmy the Jam Gent," he warned.

45

Jo spotted the lights of a cabin in the nearby woods. She pointed. "That lodge is the only building around," she said. "I bet that's where that lowlife has Dylan."

Hoisting up her clothes as best she could, Allie waddled up to the big, red-faced bus driver. "Excuse me, Mr Bus Driver, sir," she said politely through her ski mask. "We have a bit of an emergency."

"No stops scheduled for ten miles!" said the bus driver automatically. "No talking to the driver! No standing!"

Jo bent down to Timmy. "Timmy, pretend to be sick," she whispered. "Like you ate grass."

Timmy staggered to the front of the bus, pretending to retch. The bus driver looked appalled and applied his brakes with a squeal.

"Great performance, Timmy," Max whispered admiringly as they alighted from the bus. "I wish I was that good at faking it when I want to stay home from school." He launched into a terrible bout of fake vomiting. "See?" he sighed, straightening up. "You can't put in what nature left out."

The cousins, Timmy and Nicholas started off down the road and through the snowy woods towards the cabin light, which glowed and flickered between the tree trunks, beckoning them. Jo and Nicholas approached a window, Max tiptoed round to the back door and Allie headed round the side of the house.

The back door slammed open. Danny and Rufus stepped out, carrying a large bucket. The kids froze in their tracks, caught in the open like rabbits in the headlights.

Chapter Nine

Timmy sized up the situation. He started barking, and ran menacingly towards Danny and Rufus.

"Hey!" Danny shouted, stumbling backwards. "Get lost, you mutt! Go on!"

As he shooed Timmy away, the others took the opportunity to hide. Allie jumped into some bushes. Jo dragged Nicholas behind a pile of firewood. Max leaped into a nearby dustbin. Timmy stopped barking at Danny and trotted out of sight as soon as the others were safe.

Danny glared after Timmy, brushing the snow from his coat. He glanced around, before saying to Rufus: "When this is over, Nicholas will know too much. He might need to 'accidentally' fall down the well."

Rufus looked confused. "Why don't we just push him?"

Danny sighed. "Rufus," he growled, "that bucket of ash is smarter than you. Empty it and get inside."

Danny stomped back into the cabin. Shrugging, Rufus took his bucket of fireplace ash to the dustbin and tipped it in. Then he joined Danny inside.

Max emerged from the dustbin, coughing and spluttering and covered in ash as the others came out from their hiding places and looked at each other in dismay.

"We've got to find Dylan before they drop him down a well!" Allie said.

Inside the office, Dylan sat watching his computer screen. It was still showing the power station's electrical circuits, but also had a "pulse loading" bar glowing green and stating 71% complete. Bored, he examined a DVD player beside the computer, and experimentally slid his plate of anchovies into the front-load slot.

Tap tap tap.

Dylan glanced at the window. To his astonishment, Max's ash-covered face was on the other side of the glass, grinning at him. Dylan scrambled to open the latch, and moments later Max and Jo both climbed inside. Peering out, Dylan saw that they had fashioned a ladder by stacking firewood to form steps up the side of the house.

"We don't have much time," Jo said urgently, glancing around. "Nicholas has set his laptop to—" She paused and frowned at Dylan, wrinkling her nose. "Phew, you really do smell like onion."

The office door started to open, startling them. Max dived behind the desk, and Dylan hurried back to his chair, while Jo scurried behind a stuffed, three-metre Kodiak bear.

Danny and Rufus stepped into the room.

"All right, Nick," Danny said without preamble. "Time to do your stuff."

Dylan swallowed. "All right . . ." he said. "Well . . . here goes . . . my stuff."

The "pulse loading" bar now read 100%. Wincing, Dylan tentatively clicked on the mouse. The room was plunged into darkness.

"Perfect!" came Danny's voice in the gloom.

"Power's out." He turned on a torch and shone it on Dylan. His smile was unpleasant. "Just one bit of business to finish up," he said softly. "Come downstairs with me, Nick."

Behind Danny and Rufus, the huge stuffed Kodiak bear rushed forward, propelled by Jo. Danny and Rufus turned to see the snarling bear looming over them.

"Ooof," Jo puffed, pushing as hard as she could.

"Aaagghh!" Danny and Rufus screamed as Jo pushed the bear over on top of them.

As the two men struggled, Max, Jo and Dylan seized their chance and raced from the room. They sped down the stairs and out of the front door. Moments later, Danny and Rufus raced after them.

Danny burst outside with a snarl. From her hiding place behind the door, Allie stuck a ski-pole out at ankle level. Danny tumbled straight over it, landing face-first in the snow just as Rufus crashed into him from behind. Allie fled as the panting villains got to their feet and stared around wildly. A brown, black and white blur jumped over and knocked them flat again, before sitting firmly on top of them.

As Timmy sat on the thieves, the others put on the skis they had brought with them. Jo, Dylan and Allie edged over a slope and skied away down the hill.

"You don't have skis, Nicholas," Max said, clipping his boots into place. "Hop on – you're riding with me."

Nicholas clambered on to Max's back and clung on, inadvertently covering Max's eyes with his hands and causing Max to ski round in circles once or twice before heading downhill backwards. Barking joyfully, Timmy leaped off his winded prisoners and took off down the hill after them.

Danny and Rufus staggered to their feet again, their ears ringing with Nicholas's whoops and laughter as he and Max skied out of sight. In the distance, they could hear shouts and clanging and strange explosions.

"Listen," Danny said, cocking his head. "The blackout must've caused rioting down in the village. We'll be able to grab those kids back before anyone knows what's going on."

"I bet the Squid Gang's just waltzing out of prison right now," said Rufus happily as he followed

Danny towards the edge of the slope. "Though if I know Stan," he added, "he's doing a fox-trot. Very light on his feet for a morbidly obese gentleman."

They reached the edge of the slope. In the valley below, the village was brightly lit, its street full of happy people. Bells were ringing, and fireworks exploded across the velvety sky.

Danny turned red with fury. "Nick double-crossed us!" he screamed. "He only cut the power to the house – nowhere else!"

"That's not a riot in the village," said Rufus slowly. "They're having their snow festival." He stared for a moment, then beamed. "Ooh – we could get sausages . . ."

Danny strode over to a snowy tarpaulin and ripped it away, revealing two parked snowmobiles.

"I don't know who those brats are," Danny snarled as he and Rufus mounted the snowmobiles and gunned the engines. "But they're all going to pay . . ."

Chapter Ten

The kids hurtled down the dark, snowy hill on their skis, with Timmy galloping alongside. They could hear the roar of Danny and Rufus's snowmobiles in hot pursuit, just behind them. Grimly, Jo ducked under a low-hanging tree limb, while beside her Dylan jumped over a snow-covered bush.

"Max!" Nicholas called out in warning, peering over Max's shoulder. "Look out!"

Still struggling to see, Max walloped straight into a snowbank and pulled Nicholas right through to the other side.

Allie zipped past Max and Nicholas. A family of rabbits suddenly hopped into her path. She swerved to avoid them, lost her balance and started rolling downhill like a giant woolly snowball. Allie, Max and Nicholas, Jo and Dylan, all plunged to the bottom of the hill, landing on a frozen pond that gleamed in the moonlight. Unable to steer, they skied – or, in Allie's case, rolled – across the ice as best they could, spinning and whirling and barely keeping their balance until finally, they all crashed into a wall of snow on the far side of the pond.

The roar of the snowmobiles was getting closer.

"They're too fast on those snowmobiles," Jo panted, struggling to her feet. "They'll catch us before we get to the village."

Allie took a deep breath. "They won't catch us all if I wipe out in the snow and they stop to grab me," she said bravely. "I can barely move in all these clothes anyway – I'm slowing you guys up."

Timmy growled his disapproval of Allie's idea.

"We can't leave you here alone," Max protested.

"Anybody have any better ideas?" Allie demanded.

They looked at each other grimly. No one spoke.

* * *

Moments later, Danny and Rufus roared up on their snowmobiles. Danny spotted Allie lying motionless in the snow. He and Rufus slowed to a stop and dismounted.

"Well, we've got one of 'em, anyway," said Danny with grim satisfaction. He poked Allie. "C'mon, kid – you're nicked." He poked again. "Kid?" Unwrapping the bundle of clothes, he stared in dismay. "Hey, there's no kid here! It's just clothes!"

As he got to his feet beside Rufus, Max and Jo skied out of the darkness, each holding one end of a long, stout tree branch. The branch walloped Danny and Rufus neatly from behind, and brought them down in a tangled heap.

Dylan, Nicholas and Allie, shivering and clad only in jeans and T-shirt, emerged from nearby bushes and surveyed their motionless pursuers.

"OK," Allie admitted. "That was a better idea."

Acting fast, they lashed Danny and Rufus to trees, using Allie's excess clothes for ropes. Timmy grabbed one in his mouth to pull a knot extra tight.

"This should hold them till the authorities from

the village get here," said Dylan.

Danny groggily opened one eye and stared around.

"Name the kings of England," Dylan suggested. "It helps pass the time."

Danny opened his mouth and hissed: "I'm going to get you all for this, you little—"

But he got no further as Nicholas shoved an onion in his mouth.

"You're all right, Nicholas," said Jo approvingly, patting him on the back.

"So," Max said in a serious voice as they stared at their captives. "Until the police show up, we're in charge."

Dylan wagged a finger at his cousin. "Oh no we're not," he said. "We have much more important things to do." He produced a snowball from beneath his coat and threw it at Jo. "SNOWBALL FIGHT!"

And everyone pitched into a headlong snow battle, with Timmy barking joyfully among them and ducking the white missiles every time.

Epilogue

"Sticky Situation Number Fourteen," said Dylan, adjusting his camera and stamping his feet in the snow, the following day. "Brrrr! Wooo, Brrrr!"

The cousins were standing in a clearing in the woods. All around them, the tree boughs were heavy with pure white snow, and the air was silent and frozen.

"If you're stuck out in the snow, you can build a shelter and keep warm," Jo announced to the camera. "Pile up snow about three metres across and two metres high."

Max and Timmy obediently piled snow into a heap beside Jo. Dylan kept track on his viewfinder.

"Then hollow it out," Jo continued, "and save that snow for your entrance tunnel."

Max and Timmy dug the snow out from the middle of the pile, creating a second smaller pile beside the first.

"Hollow that out as an entrance tunnel," Jo said.

Now looking more than a little winded, Max and Timmy repeated the hollowing-out process, creating a low entrance tunnel to the larger shelter.

"And you'll have a cosy shelter to protect you from the elements," Jo concluded.

"And if Allie's your cousin," Max panted, "you'll have a hot bath to recuperate in, too."

He and Timmy crossed the clearing to Allie, who was relaxing in a steaming bathtub beneath a particularly snowy tree and eating a turkey drumstick. Dylan swung his camera round.

Allie smiled at the lens and waved her drumstick. "Knowing the number of a good carry-out food place is helpful, too," she advised happily.

LOOK OUT FOR THE WHOLE SERIES!

THE CASE OF THE THIEF WHO
DRINKS FROM THE TOILET

**Hodder
Children's
Books**

A division of Hachette Children's Books

Special thanks to Lucy Courtenay
and Artful Doodlers

First published in Great Britain in 2008 by Hodder Children's Books

1

A Catalogue record for this book is available from the British Library

ISBN 978 0 340 95979 4

Typeset in Weiss by Avon DataSet Ltd,
Bidford on Avon, Warwickshire

Printed in Great Britain by
Clays Ltd, St Ives plc

The paper and board used in this paperback by Hodder Children's
Books are natural recyclable products made from wood grown in
sustainable forests. The manufacturing processes conform to the
environmental regulations of the country of origin.

Hodder Children's Books
a division of Hachette Children's Books
338 Euston Road, London NW1 3BH
An Hachette Livre UK Company
www.hachettelivre.co.uk

Chapter One

"Whoooo!"

The four Kirrin cousins pelted down the steep pavement on a homemade street-sled, weaving in and out of lamp-posts, dustbins and pedestrians. A handsome black, brown and white dog tore on ahead of them.

"Timmy," Jo yelled, her dark brown hair whipping round her face, "don't get too far ahead! I don't want you getting lost!"

They flew around a corner, steering a little helplessly. Mrs Kluck, a local Falcongate resident, had the misfortune to be hurrying along the pavement carrying groceries. Unwittingly, she

stepped straight into the path of the sled. Seeing the kids approaching at speed, she froze.

"Go to the right, Mrs Kluck!" Dylan yelled, straightening his skew-whiff glasses with one hand as he steered left with the other.

Mrs Kluck frantically moved to her right, her eyes still glued to the fast-approaching sled.

"No!" yelled Max. His blond fringe stood straight up in the oncoming wind. "*Our* right!"

The cousins turned harder to their left. Mrs Kluck ran a little faster, still heading to *her* right.

CRASSHH!

Everyone skidded at once into a pile of autumn leaves that had been carefully raked into a pile on the pavement by a quiet-looking gentleman. The gentlemen studied the crash quizzically, then started raking all over again.

"Sorry about that, Mrs Kluck," Allie panted, brushing leaves off her long blond hair. "We zigged when you zagged."

"Quick, help me up," said Mrs Kluck feebly, holding out her hand to Max. "My Smidgie!"

"I don't know what your Smidgie is," Max said, taking her hand carefully, "but if you injured it you

might not want to get up right away."

"Smidgie is my precious puppy!" Mrs Kluck wailed.

Max struggled to help the generously built woman to her feet, but Mrs Kluck tumbled back into the leaves.

"Oooh!" Mrs Kluck squealed.

With a sigh, the tight-lipped gentleman resumed his raking for a third time.

"Here," Jo offered, staring around at the scattered shopping, "let us get your groceries." She hunkered down to examine something. "I hope you like omelettes," she added, and lifted a carton of eggs that were liberally seeping egg yolks.

"I lost track of time gossiping in the shop," Mrs Kluck exclaimed, struggling to get to her feet, "and Smidgie needs to be fed at precise times during the day. Oooh . . ."

Mrs Kluck tumbled back into the leaves once again. The raking gentleman turned a delicate shade of puce, and began moving his rake a little more fiercely. Dylan joined Max to help hoist the woman up, while Allie scrambled around on the pavement with Jo, picking up the groceries.

3

". . . otherwise he has bad dreams about being chased by vengeful postmen," Mrs Kluck continued, still talking about her puppy. She almost overbalanced for the fourth time, but the gentleman with the rake was quick on the uptake and managed to prop her up before she hit his leaves again.

"Oooo-K," said Jo, standing up with her arms full of shopping. "Well, there's your house. Why don't we come in and—" She peered into the grocery bag and grimaced— "glue your crackers back together."

"She's nimble for an older woman," Dylan observed, as the cousins followed the wheezing, trotting lady to the door of her flat.

Jo opened the door for Mrs Kluck and looked inside. "Um," she said, hefting the shopping into a more comfortable position, "do you have furniture, Mrs Kluck?"

"Of course," Mrs Kluck replied in surprise.

"Then I'm afraid you've been robbed," Jo said.

She opened the door wider to reveal Mrs Kluck's flat. The whole place was empty.

"Ooooh . . ." Mrs Kluck made a funny gasping noise and fainted backwards into Dylan's arms.

4

Dylan tried his best to hold her up. "She's heavy, too . . ." he wheezed as he sank under Mrs Kluck's weight.

Chapter Two

Jo, Allie and Max quickly scanned the flat while Dylan struggled to prop up the semi-conscious Mrs Kluck.

"Another robbery?" Jo frowned. "This is the third one in Falcongate this week."

"Check for clues," Max said. "Anything out of the ordinary."

"I'm getting squashed here," panted Dylan as the others pushed past him and went inside the flat. "That's not ordinary."

Allie ran back with a magazine to fan Mrs Kluck. "Ooh, I hope her Smidgie's all right," she said anxiously.

"Smidgie!" shouted Mrs Kluck, pushing out of Dylan's arms and standing bolt upright before darting into the flat.

"Looks like they got all the furniture," Jo said, staring around the empty living room.

"They're valuable antiques!" Mrs Kluck wailed, pressing her hands to her face. "Smidgie – where are you?" She paled. "Oh! Check the biscuit jar!"

In the kitchen, Max checked a biscuit jar. "He's not in here," he said, staring sadly at the empty insides. "And the robbers got all the biscuits. These are bad, bad people."

"That jar's where I hide all my money!" Mrs Kluck screamed. "It's all gone!"

"So then," said Max, glancing around the flat with interest, "maybe she keeps some biscuits in the pantry . . ."

"I don't see Smidgie!" shouted Mrs Kluck, wild-eyed and running around the flat like a frantic hen. "What if they got him too?!"

"Maybe he ran out when the thieves came in," Allie suggested.

Mrs Kluck looked a little calmer. "If he just ran off, I can find him," she said hopefully. "He has an

ID chip in his shoulder – the vet just put it there."

Timmy sniffed at a small drawer in a cupboard tucked into the corner. Then he barked. Jo ran to open the drawer. Inside was a tiny puppy, shivering and blinking up at her.

Jo smiled broadly, and patted Timmy on the neck. "Who needs an ID chip when you've got Timmy?" she said.

Mrs Kluck rushed to the drawer and scooped out the puppy. "Smidgie!!" she gasped, covering the little dog with kisses. "Oh my little cupcake! Who's the most wonderful dog in the whole wide world?"

"Well," said Jo in a low voice to Allie, "Timmy is, but Mrs Kluck's had a tough day." she knelt down and took Timmy's shaggy head in her hands. "Don't you ever get lost, Timmy," she instructed. "I couldn't stand it."

"Oh, my little Smidgie widgie," Mrs Kluck crooned, nuzzling her puppy shamelessly.

"Ew," said Allie.

"Yuk," Jo agreed, watching Mrs Kluck with a revolted expression on her face. "Tell me about it."

Allie shook her head. "No," she said. "I mean –

look. I think the thieves scared Smidgie so much that he . . . dropped something."

She pointed at a little black pellet lying on some newspaper on the floor beside Smidgie's water dish. Max picked up the pellet and popped it in his mouth.

"Gross!" shouted Jo, Allie and Dylan, all looking appalled.

"Un-gross," Max corrected. "It's black liquorice."

"Double gross!!" Dylan shrieked. "What?" he protested as the others looked at him. "I prefer red. It's the perfect food."

"I don't care for it in any colour," said Mrs Kluck, caressing Smidgie. "That's why I never keep any in my house."

There was a pause. Jo flung up her hand and pointed at Max.

"Wait!" she said. "The robbers might have left that! You're eating evidence!"

Max stopped mid-chew as Jo thrust her hand into his mouth and removed the liquorice.

"Great," said Dylan, staring at the pulpy mass in Jo's fingers. "The fingerprints got all sucked off."

"Try checking my tongue for prints," Max

suggested, sticking his tongue out. "Quick!" he mumbled. "Before they dissolve!"

He whipped out a magnifying glass and offered it to his cousins. When no one took the magnifying glass from him, he tried to check his own tongue, without success.

"Maybe we should look around town for someone with black teeth," said Allie. "Like that undead guy in the zombie movie." She put on a zombie face, extended her arms and shuffled around.

"You look like my grandfather heading for the loo in the middle of the night," said Max, lowering the magnifying glass.

The cousins stared at Mrs Kluck and Smidgie. They were wrapped in a blissful cuddle, crooning at each other. It was a very soppy sight.

"I think these two want to be alone," Jo observed.

The Five crept out of the flat, leaving Mrs Kluck and Smidgie. Allie paused in front of a wonky picture and straightened it surreptitiously, before following the others outside.

Chapter Three

In Falcongate's sweet shop, the cousins stood across from old Mr Fedgewick, the sweet-shop proprietor. Mr Fedgewick had been selling sweets in Falcongate for as long as anyone could remember, and was almost completely deaf.

"So," Mr Fedgewick said in a quavery voice, adjusting his hearing aid. "You want to know who's been in my sweet shop to purchase black little fish, eh?"

"No," said Jo loudly. "Black *liquorice*. Anybody you can remember."

"Ah," said Mr Fedgewick, his face clearing. "Black liquorice. Yes. Well, my memory isn't what it

used to be, so I'll really have to concentrate."

He cupped his gnarled old hands over his eyes, apparently to block out any visual distractions. As he thought, his cat strolled on to the shop floor from the back room. It eyed Timmy with disgust.

"Now let's see," Mr Fedgewick said from behind his hands. "I remember a fellow just the other day. Now what did he say his name was?"

Timmy wagged a greeting at the cat. The cat hissed and swatted Timmy's nose. Affronted, Timmy dropped his friendly approach and proceeded to chase the cat all round the shop.

"Timmy!" Dylan called, setting off after the animals.

"No," Mr Falcongate said consideringly, still with his eyes behind his hands. "The name wasn't Timmy. It was something more like . . ."

CRASH!

The cat knocked over a meticulously organised display of sweets, sticks of rock, bags of toffee and trays of chocolate. They hit the floor in a multicoloured mess.

"Rwoof!" Timmy barked

"No, it wasn't Ruth," Mr Fedgewick tutted,

amazingly oblivious to the mayhem. "I said it was a fellow. Can't you hear?"

A jar of gobstoppers crashed to the ground, scattering like marbles and making the shop floor as treacherous as an ice rink. The cat leaped on to a high shelf, pursued ambitiously by Timmy. It knocked over a big jar of jelly beans, which streamed down into Max's waiting mouth.

"I had a dream like this once," mumbled Max happily through his jelly beans.

Timmy was now chasing the cat towards a huge slab of toffee. The cat attempted to barrel straight through it, but the toffee stretched like a rubber band and snapped back, hurling the cat straight out of the open front door.

"Timmy!" Jo shouted as Timmy shot out of the door in hot pursuit. "Get back here!"

"You keep thinking, Mr Fedgewick," called Allie politely, following the others as they dashed out of the door after Timmy. "We'll get back to you . . ."

"You can't keep running off like this!" Jo panted, catching up with Timmy as he chased Mr Fedgewick's cat up a tree. "You'll get lost one day."

"Maybe Timmy could use one of those ID chips," Dylan suggested.

Timmy stopped barking at the cat for an instant and perked up.

"ID chips, Timmy," Dylan repeated. "Not fish and chips."

"Ooh, fish and chips," said Max as Timmy grumbled in disapproval and went back to torturing the cat. "I'm hungry. Who's hungry?"

Half an hour later, the kids were in Falcongate's local veterinary surgery, getting Timmy fitted with an ID chip. The vet's name was Dr Prudelock, and he was doing his best to get near Timmy with the syringe containing the chip. Timmy growled a warning as Dr Prudelock pushed his extremely shiny glasses up his sweaty nose and tried to approach Timmy's shoulder from a different angle.

"Settle down, boy," Jo said, stroking Timmy. "I know he's new around here, but you can trust him."

"He's got a lot of diplomas, Timmy," Max said earnestly, gazing at the framed certificates decorating the surgery walls. "That must mean something."

Dr Prudelock was using his most soothing manner as he spoke to Timmy. "We'll just insert this little chippie-wippie into your shoulder-woulder," he said in a sing-song voice, "and—"

"Woof!"

Timmy barked loudly. Dr Prudelock recoiled.

"I guess Timmy got up on the wrong side of the dog bed this morning," Dylan said.

Jo tried to hold Timmy, but he continually wrestled his way free. Before long, he had ended up straddling Jo's head as Dr Prudelock waved his syringe hopelessly in the background.

"Maybe I'll bring him back another day," Jo panted in a squashed sort of voice.

"Maybe after he's had a big lunch," Max said. "That always makes me sleepy."

Embarrassed, Jo exited with the struggling Timmy.

"We're sorry to have wasted your time," Allie said politely as she started out of the surgery after the others.

Dr Prudelock mopped his sweaty forehead. "I am a busy man," he said peevishly. An odd expression crossed his face, and he added in a more polite tone

of voice: "But you could do me a favour ..."

Indicating that Allie, Max and Dylan should follow him, he led them into a room next to his surgery. It was lined wall-to-wall with animal cages.

"How about adopting one of these abandoned pets?" said Dr Prudelock in a slightly sinister voice as the kids stared around the room in amazement. "I think every house should have one of my special animals . . ."

"Cute little bunnies!" Allie gasped, her eyes lighting up as she visited each animal in its cage. "Cute little kittens – ooh, kissy kissy! Cute little birdies! Cheep cheep—"

She stopped at the next cage and gawped at the small, hairy monkey inside. It eyed her malevolently and screeched.

"Loud screechy monkey!" Allie said, trying to maintain the cute factor in her voice and failing miserably.

Unlike Allie, Max and Dylan both lit up with enthusiasm.

"A monkey?" they said, rushing over to the cage. "All right!" They strutted in front of the cage and started chanting: "Mon-key! Mon-key! Mon-key!"

Allie frowned. She had a horrible feeling that they were about to get to know the monkey a little better than she would have liked.

Chapter Four

"Why did we have to choose a monkey?" Allie complained as they all walked back to Jo's house with Max and Dylan's new friend riding on Max's shoulder.

Max stared at Allie like she was talking Chinese. "Because – *it's a monkey!*" he said.

"But . . . isn't it wrong to keep monkeys as pets?" Allie persisted.

"I suppose so," Max said reluctantly. "But he needs a home until we can find a better place for him."

"Ooh!" said Dylan. "Till then, we could hire him out as a commercial mascot." He broke into song, composing sample jingles as he went along: "Don't

monkey around, we have the best cars in town . . .
Don't monkey around, we have the best food in
town . . . Don't monkey around, we have the best
DIY in town . . ."

The monkey snatched Dylan's cap and put it on
his head.

"Or he'd make a good pickpocket," said Max,
looking impressed. "Little guy's got quick hands."

The monkey grabbed Allie's bag, found her lip
gloss and smeared it all over its face.

"Hey!" Allie complained. "They may be quick, but they don't know how to apply lip gloss."

The monkey leaned down and smeared lip gloss all over Max.

"Although he's learning . . ." Allie conceded.

Over at Jo's house, Jo's dad Ravi was working underneath his valuable, beautifully restored 1932 Kranzler-Ross convertible, his feet protruding from beneath it. Jo sat nearby, handing him tools.

"Thanks, Jo," said Ravi, taking the tools and tinkering happily under the convertible's chassis. "This is one of only three 1932 Kranzler-Rosses left in the world. Winston Churchill got car-sick in the back seat."

"That's great, Dad," Jo said absently. She was thinking out loud. "So, whoever robbed Mrs Kluck knew exactly what she had that was valuable, where it was hidden, and that she'd be out for fifteen minutes for her daily shopping," she murmured to herself, handing her dad a spanner. "How is that possible?"

A strange person leaped out in front of Jo wearing a scary wooden mask.

"Booga-booga!" shrieked the person behind the mask.

"Wahhhh!" Jo scrambled to her feet in terror.

Jo's mother George removed the mask, looking pleased. "Excellent," George said happily. "I was afraid for a moment it wasn't scary enough. It's a witch doctor's mask from the Solomon Islands. They used it to scare sickness out of people."

"Well, it scared *something* out of me," Jo said, sitting down again with her hand held over her heart.

"I'm going to donate it to the Old Sailors' home for their auction," George explained, turning the mask carefully around in her hands and studying it from all angles. "It's a priceless antique – they can raise money for exercise equipment."

Out of nowhere, a small hairy monkey leaped on to George's back and screeched.

"Though that would get their hearts going pretty well, too . . ." said George faintly as the monkey scrambled around on her shoulders.

"Down Chance!" Max called, strolling round the corner with Dylan and Allie. "Here, monkey, monkey . . ."

21

The monkey jumped nimbly off George and returned to Max's shoulder.

"Chance needed a home, so we adopted him," Dylan explained proudly. "I'm going to teach him to make my bed."

"They named him 'Chance' because there's a very good chance he'll break something," Allie said, sounding unimpressed.

Timmy stared at the monkey. His hackles rose and he growled suspiciously.

"Well, look who's jealous of the newest member of the family," Max grinned.

Chance seized a small stone in his wizened fist and threw it at Timmy. It hit Timmy on the nose.

"Owwooo," Timmy howled.

In a flash, Timmy was chasing Chance around the old convertible.

"Keep them out of the front seat!!" Ravi shouted. "Winston Churchill choked on a chicken bone in that seat!"

Chance bolted away with Timmy hot on his tail, followed by the four kids and George. Taking a flying leap at the washing line, the monkey grabbed hold of the line and started zipping along it hand-

over hand, while Timmy followed along the ground below, barking like mad.

"Timmy started it," Dylan panted, chasing both animals. "He's obviously jealous. I mean, Chance can open a tin of kippers with his feet."

"Why'd you bring home something smelly and obnoxious?" Jo complained to Allie in a low voice. "We've already got Dylan."

The sky started raining clothes pegs as Chance hurled handfuls of them at Timmy. When the monkey reached the end of the washing line, the line broke and dropped Chance, the line and the laundry down in the mud. Undeterred, Chance kept running, the line travelling with him. The far end of the line wrapped around Ravi's leg, which was still sticking out from beneath the old car. Before Ravi could react, the clothes line was pulling him out and Chance was dragging him along on his wheeled mechanic's creeper-board, laundry on top of his head and torso.

"I'm being dragged by a monkey with laundry on my face," Ravi shouted, his voice muffled with pants and vests as the creeper-board scooted along at a dangerous speed. "The fortune teller was right!"

Chance's next means of escape was the large ride-on lawnmower. He jumped aboard and gunned the engine, driving in erratic circles and twisting Ravi deeper and deeper into the laundry.

"Oohhhh," Ravi moaned, thrashing his hands around.

The kids leaped out of the way as Chance careened across the garden, cutting weird patterns in the grass and crashing through a patio table with a bowl of punch on it. The bowl flew into the air and landed on George.

"Oooooo," George shrieked, soaked in punch.

At last, the mower cut the clothesline. Ravi's wheeled board rolled to a stop as Chance sped off into the woods, with the cousins and George still in hot pursuit.

"See?" Dylan shouted in delight, pelting after the others. "He can mow lawns! This monkey's worth a fortune!"

Twenty minutes later, the Kirrins were still searching for Chance and the mower deep in the woods.

"Chance!" Max bellowed through cupped hands. "Chance!"

They were startled by the deep and distinctive *vroom!* of an engine high above them.

"I forget," said Dylan, sniffing the air. "Do birds give off exhaust fumes?"

Everyone looked up to see the ride-on mower lodged in a high tree. Chance was still in the driver's seat, clapping with delight.

"You're a very naughty monkey!" George shouted crossly. "Get that mower down here this instant!"

"Bad choice of words, Mum," said Jo, dashing for cover. "Run!"

They all scattered as the mower crashed down out of the tree and splintered on the ground.

Having finally captured the monkey, the cousins and George trudged back to the house. Chance was riding on Max's shoulder again, looking peaceful. Ravi was lying in the middle of the lawn on his wheeled mechanic's board, his head and torso still covered with laundry.

"Ravi, dear," George said, hurrying over to her husband. "Are you all right?"

"Just thought I'd nap till the monkey came home," Ravi said faintly.

As his legs started to stir, the kids continued on towards the barn beside Jo's house. Jo stared. Her heart sank.

"Oh no . . ." she said. "Dad, your car . . ."

"What about it?" Ravi said, peeling laundry stiffly off his head.

"It's been stolen!" Jo cried.

Chapter Five

"Thanks for coming, you Kirrins," Mr Fedgewick quavered, back in the sweet shop later in the day. "I went skydiving this afternoon. Always clears my head."

Jo, Max, Allie and Dylan glanced at each other, picturing Mr Fedgewick hurtling through the air at a hundred miles an hour and making notes as he fell.

"I came up with all the names of people who have bought black liquorice from me recently," Mr Fedgewick continued.

He handed the cousins an enormously long piece of paper.

"This is a million names," said Dylan, dumbfounded.

"Fiona Finnyfrock," Allie giggled, reading the list over Dylan's shoulder. "There's someone named 'Fiona Finnyfrock'!"

As the Five examined the list, Mr Fedgewick's Airedale terrier ambled into the room. Naturally, Timmy noticed him first. Giving a growl, Timmy flew at the Airedale and tore off its collar.

Looking flustered, Jo grabbed Timmy and tore the Airedale's collar away from him. "Sorry, Mr Fedgewick," she apologised, stuffing the collar into her pocket. "I don't know what's got into Timmy lately."

Mr Fedgewick shuffled out from behind the sweet counter and examined his dog a little anxiously. "Oh, Caesar's all right," he said, straightening up. "Your dog only went after the collar, and it was a free sample from that Dr Prudelock."

"Still, we'll get the collar fixed, don't you worry," Max promised. "And if you feel like rewarding us with unlimited peanut brittle," he added hopefully, "well, that's your affair."

"And whatever's got into Timmy, we're going to get it taken care of once and for all," said Jo, holding firmly on to Timmy's collar. "Shame on you, Timmy," she said, and tugged Timmy out of the shop. Timmy whimpered, but followed his mistress obediently.

Out on the pavement, the Five looked at one another. Behaving so aggressively wasn't like Timmy at all. What was the matter with Jo's dog?

"You can't blame this one on Chance," Max said, speaking into the silence. "He's been waiting out here, good as gold. I left him tied to that post."

He pointed across to a sign post, which had a tether lashed to it. All eyes followed the tether from the sign post, across the pavement and up the nearby set of painters' scaffolding to the monkey sitting on the very top. With a wicked grin, Chance weighed the large pot of paint in his little paws before dumping the whole lot on the Five's heads.

"Aaargh!"

Everyone leaped out of the way – too late – dripping from head to toe with paint.

"OK," Max spluttered, wiping paint out of his eyes, "that one you can blame on Chance."

* * *

Back at the vet's surgery, Jo explained to Dr Prudelock what Timmy had done, as the others looked on.

"Hmm . . ." Dr Prudelock said, looking a little shifty. "He, um, he tore that collar right off Mr Fedgewick's Airedale?"

Jo lifted up the broken collar and nodded.

"Well, er . . ." said Dr Prudelock, eyeing Timmy carefully, "maybe something in his diet is, um, causing an imbalance. I'll keep him overnight to run some testy-westies."

Dr Prudelock's receptionist took Timmy gingerly from Jo. Timmy tried to fight her off, twisting and growling in her arms. Jo blinked back the tears as the receptionist wrestled Timmy out of the room.

"And I could fix that collar for you too," Dr Prudelock continued. "Here, give it to me—"

Dr Prudelock made to snatch the broken collar from Jo. But Chance leaped from Max's shoulder and snatched the collar first.

"All this monkey business is wiping me out," Max said wearily, as Chance scampered out of the surgery with the collar.

"Hey," Dylan said, struck by an idea as he followed Max and the others after Chance. "There's another way we can make money out of him – as a personal trainer!"

Running down the pavement after his cousins, Dylan happily imagined an aerobics class, with Chance in full Lycra leading Uncle Ravi and Constable Stubblefield in a wild series of exercises, which included a bout of swinging on a set of light fixtures – that brought the ceiling down!

"So," Dylan added reluctantly to himself,

dodging round a pair of surprised pedestrians on the pavement, "that plan has a few kinks to work out . . ."

Still clutching the broken collar, Chance led the cousins a merry dance all the way back to Jo's house. He scampered into George's study and leaped up on top of a bookcase beside the scary Solomon Islands' witch-doctor mask. He grinned down at Max and Dylan as they crashed through the door, puffing and winded.

"OK, Chance," Dylan gasped, holding his sides as Jo and Allie ran into the study to join them, "game's up. Toss the collar. With your feet, if possible," he added hopefully, "because I can't get enough of that thumb-on-the-foot stuff you monkeys do."

Chance seized a book and tossed it down, hitting Max on the forehead. This was followed by a globe, which caught Dylan on the temple. The witch-doctor mask was Chance's masterstroke, as it landed neatly over Max's head. Unable to help themselves, Jo and Allie started laughing as Max stumbled around the room in a dizzy witch-doctor dance.

"Come on down, you sweet little thing, you," Allie giggled, holding out her arms to Chance.

Charmed, the monkey leaped down from the bookcase and landed on Allie's shoulder. Allie effortlessly took the broken collar from his little paws and handed it to Jo, throwing a smug look at the boys for good measure.

"Seems like he didn't monkify it too badly . . ." Jo said, studying the collar carefully. She frowned. "Hey, wait a second – Dylan, take a look at this . . ." Grabbing a magnifying glass from a nearby drawer, Jo handed it to Dylan along with the collar. "You're the tech guy," Jo continued. "What's the deal with that stud in the collar?"

"It's not a stud," Dylan said in surprise, staring at the collar through the magnifying glass. "It's a micro video camera."

Now it was Max's turn to frown. "Didn't Mr Fedgewick say he got this collar from Dr Prudelock?" he asked.

"Yeah," said Allie thoughtfully. "And Dr Prudelock seemed awfully eager to get it from us."

"Sounds as if it's time for another surgery visit," Jo declared, taking the collar back from Dylan. "A

monkey-less surgery visit," she added firmly to Max. "Chance is a little too much like having our own, personal hurricane."

Chapter Six

Down at Dr Prudelock's surgery, the front entrance was firmly locked.

"Closed?" Dylan said in surprise, tugging at the handle. "It's mid-afternoon. I think I'll be a vet – you hardly ever work."

Jo studied the front of the surgery. She spotted an open window, and motioned the others towards it.

"Prudelock's up to something," she said, putting her foot on the wall. "And he's got my dog in there. So I'm declaring him open for business."

They all climbed in through the window to the surgery's reception area. Jo landed lightly on her

feet and dusted off her hands.

"I'm going to find Timmy," she said, starting off across the surgery floor towards the back of the clinic. "You guys look for anything unusual."

"There's something unusual," said Allie in a soppy voice, pointing at a cage of rabbits on the floor. "Unusually cute!'"

Max and Dylan looked perplexed as Allie rushed over to the rabbits and started cooing at them through the bars.

"The three adorablest bunnies who ever lived," Allie gushed, waggling her fingers at the rabbits. "Hi, there little bunnies! Who's adorable? 'I'm adorable, Allie! Hop, hop, hop!'"

Allie started hopping around the room like a rabbit.

"Well," said Dylan to Max after a strained pause, "we can keep watching her, or check what's in that room." He gestured towards a door.

With one last gaze at Allie making smoochy faces at the rabbits, Max and Dylan slipped through the door in question. They gazed around in astonishment. One entire room was covered with a bank of video monitors. They all seemed to be

showing the interiors of different homes.

"Wow," Dylan murmured, "that's quite an entertainment system. I tell you, these vets have a sweet, sweet gig."

"But they've got lousy shows," Max pointed out, staring at the endless pictures of living- and dining-rooms. "It's like they're all tuned to the Boring Channel."

Dylan studied the screens more closely. One of the monitors was showing a cat's-eye view of a birdcage. Leaning in from the side of the picture came a paw, trying its best to reach through the birdcage bars.

"It's as if every monitor is showing things through the eyes of . . . housepets . . ." Dylan said.

He glanced down at another monitor, which showed a kitchen counter from the point of view of an average-sized dog. A large, juicy, unattended steak was sitting on a plate on the counter. Suddenly the camera leaped, missed the steak, leaped again and knocked the plate to the floor.

Max and Dylan gazed around the room, mesmerised. On a screen in the far corner of the room, the camera was clearly round the neck of a

cat pursuing a mouse. The point-of-view wove between the legs of various tables and chairs like a live-action *Tom and Jerry* cartoon as the mouse sprinted along the skirting board, ducking into a hole at the last minute. The camera skidded straight into a wall with a wallop.

"Heh-heh," said Max. "Mouse won that round."

"Hey," said Allie, entering behind them and staring in surprise at a monitor near the ceiling. "How come Aunt George's study is on TV? When did she get her own show? Can I be on it? I can dance a little!"

Max and Dylan swung round and gawped at the monitor in question. It showed an image of George's study, taken from a high angle. The camera's point of view approached a vase of flowers, and a monkey paw shot into focus. The paw grabbed the vase, pulled it close as if to take a sniff, and then threw it to the ground.

"Aw, Chance," Max winced as the vase shattered. "That's going to come out of my pocket money."

"When we got Chance from Dr Prudelock, he had a collar on, right?" said Dylan, his nose almost pressed up against the screen as he watched

the view from the monkey bounding around George's study.

"So, he's wearing a microcamera like Mr Fedgewick's Airedale," Allie deduced.

"Hey," said Max, pointing at a different screen. "There's Mrs Kluck."

Mrs Kluck was looming in towards the camera, making a horrific kissy-face.

"Kids shouldn't be allowed to see that," Dylan said, shuddering and withdrawing as Mrs Kluck's lips puckered up much too close.

"So Smidgie must be wearing a camera, too," said Max triumphantly.

"Then these monitors must be transmissions from Dr Prudelock's patients," said Dylan. "He puts cameras on all of them."

Bracing himself, Dylan eyed Mrs Kluck's monitor again. Mrs Kluck was still slobbering at the camera.

"So Prudelock must be the robber," said Allie, following Dylan's gaze. "That's how he knew when Mrs Kluck wouldn't be home."

"And about Uncle Ravi's car," Max put in, "and when we weren't home. From Chance's camera." He

stared sadly at the monitor showing Chance. "Betrayed by our own monkey. Life can be cruel."

"I bet Timmy tore that Airedale's collar off because he knew something was wrong with it," Dylan guessed.

Max nodded, adding: "And it's probably why he didn't trust Dr Prudelock. Or Chance."

They looked round as Jo entered the room.

"I can't find Timmy anywhere!" Jo said. She looked worried.

They all looked at one another anxiously.

"Where could he be?" Allie asked, biting her lip.

While the Kirrins were in the surgery, a nondescript van was driving along a small country road. Dr Prudelock's receptionist sat in the driver's seat. Every now and again, she glanced in the rear-view mirror, to see if they were being followed. Beside her in the passenger seat, Dr Prudelock studied a portable monitor displaying George's empty study.

"The house will be empty for an hour," said Dr Prudelock, staring greedily at the monitor and then grinning round at his receptionist. "Perfect time to grab that priceless mask."

Dr Prudelock glanced over his shoulder into the back of the van, which contained several caged pets. His eye fell on Timmy, his expression cold. Timmy stared right back without blinking.

"And after that," Dr Prudelock said with an unpleasant laugh, "we'll deal with *Timmy*."

Chapter Seven

Max tapped Dylan on the shoulder and pointed at a monitor in the furthest corner of the room. Allie and Jo looked as well. The screen showed a dog's-eye view of Dr Prudelock in the back of his van, holding out one of his camera-equipped collars.

"All right, Skittles," came Dr Prudelock's voice. "After we grab the Kirrins' mask, we'll drop you off at your owner's. Do a good job showing us where he keeps his valuables. There's a good dog."

As Prudelock moved out of camera view, the dog-camera's gaze settled on Timmy in his cage.

"There he is!" Max, Allie, Jo and Dylan all gasped in unison. "Timmy!"

Jo's eyes narrowed with anger at the sight of Timmy's cage. She spun round and raced from the room. The others followed, wincing as Jo kicked open the locked front door and headed outside.

"I think she's a little upset," Allie said, watching as Jo powered away down the street.

"*I* think if she gets her hands on Dr Prudelock, he's going to get 'fixed'," Dylan muttered.

Half an hour later, Dr Prudelock quietly climbed out of the van and sneaked to the back of Jo's house. From the shrubbery, the four cousins watched as the vet stole up to the window of George's study and climbed inside.

"That's one doctor you just don't want making a house call," Dylan said, shaking his head.

Prudelock reappeared at the study window, clutching the mask. Jo got ready to jump out of the shrubbery and catch him in the act. But Chance got there first. As Dr Prudelock climbed back out of the window, the little monkey took a flying leap through the air and landed on the thieving vet's head, gleefully covering Dr Prudelock's eyes with his little paws.

"Get him, Chance!" Max cheered, peering through the shrubbery leaves.

"And speaking of 'chance'," Jo said, "here's ours!"

Prudelock staggered around in front of the house, trying to dislodge Chance from his head. Seizing the opportunity, the kids leaped from their hiding places and raced over.

"Ow!" moaned Dr Prudelock, banging into a wall. "Oh!"

"Hold it there, mister!" Allie shouted, aiming the

nozzle of the garden hose at the vet. "I'm not afraid to use this!"

With a snarl, Prudelock threw Chance off his head and bolted round the corner.

Allie lowered the hose. "I *told* him to hold it, but he's not holding it," she complained.

WHAM!

Prudelock ran straight into the chest of Constable Stubblefield, bringing him to a jarring stop.

"Oof," gasped Dr Prudelock.

"You know," said Constable Stubblefield severely, "the polite thing to say to a lady in a situation such as this is 'excuse me'."

Prudelock's eyes widened in panic. He tried to make another run for it, but not before Constable Stubblefield had him firmly by the collar.

"You, my man," said Constable Stubblefield, tightening her grip as Prudelock squirmed, "are nicked. I'll have that mask, please."

As Max, Jo, Allie and Dylan ran up to join the fun, Chance leaped off Max's shoulder and snatched the mask neatly from Constable Stubblefield.

"That's it, Chance," Max shouted, spinning

round as the monkey fled into the woods. "You have lost your banana privileges for a week!"

The spluttering sound of the van filled the air.

"You guys go after Chance," Jo said, darting towards the van as Dr Prudelock's receptionist struggled to start the engine. "I'm saving Timmy!"

Allie raced after Jo, leaving Dylan and Max to run after Chance as instructed. Dr Prudelock, taking advantage of the confusion, gave Constable Stubblefield a shove and made a getaway into the woods.

"Come back here, you goat-haired, duck-livered mule head!" Constable Stubblefield yelled, giving chase.

"Sorry," Dr Prudelock shouted back, leaping nimbly into the undergrowth. "I'm afraid I need to get that mask, since I'll be fleeing the country today!"

And as Constable Stubblefield watched in dismay, the vet disappeared into the trees and was gone.

Allie and Jo sprinted up to the van just as the receptionist got the engine started. They opened

the rear doors and flung themselves inside as the van roared away.

"Woof!" Timmy barked joyfully as the girls slammed the van doors shut behind them.

"Timmy!" Jo said in delight. Timmy panted happily at her through the bars of his cage. "Oh Timmy, you're all right!"

"No use trying to escape," Allie called through to the driver's seat. "We're here. Might as well pull over!"

In response, the receptionist pulled hard left on the steering wheel, sending Allie and Jo sliding across the van with all the animal cages sliding along beside them.

"Ooof," Allie gasped, banging against the van wall.

Jo reached to undo the lock on Timmy's cage. Freed, Timmy bounded to the front of the van to get right in the receptionist's face and give her a good, menacing growl.

"GRRRR!"

"Actually," said the receptionist weakly, "pulling over sounds like a fine idea."

Chapter Eight

Back in the woods, Chance was leading the field by a comfortable margin. Max and Dylan puffed after him, gasping for breath and trying not to stumble over the hidden roots and branches underfoot.

Now wearing the mask, Chance veered off the path and leaped up into a tree. There was nothing for it. Max and Dylan pulled themselves wearily up the tree after the monkey. Chance grinned cheekily at them as they struggled to a high branch, then leaped for a vine and swung away.

"Not fair!" Dylan gasped, holding his sides and watching as Chance flew towards a different tree. "He's a monkey!"

Max spotted some vines nearby. "We can tie these on to the limbs," he said confidently. He tried and failed to tie a bowline knot round the tree limb where he and Dylan were now sitting. "Let's see . . ." he said, looking confused as he stared at the vine in his hand. "How do the Scouts remember it? . . . 'The rabbit comes round the hole and behind the tree . . .'"

"No," Dylan corrected, taking a vine, "it's *behind* the hole and *round* the tree . . ."

"Now wait," Max said, holding his finger up. "Was it a *rabbit* that went round the hole and behind the tree?"

Dylan tugged and heaved at his vine knot. "*Behind* the hole," he repeated, struggling to get the vine to hold around the branch. "*Round* the tree."

Max wasn't listening. "Maybe it was a squirrel . . ." he said thoughtfully.

Dylan noticed Chance disappearing into the distance, the mask still firmly on his little monkey head. "Would you just tie it and *go?!*" he demanded.

Max scrambled to fix his knot the same way as Dylan. They both grabbed their respective vines and jumped.

"Whaaaaaaaaaaaaaa!"

Somehow they made it safely to the next tree. Elated, they clapped each other on the back. Then they realised that Chance was even further ahead than before. They glanced around in desperation for some way of travelling to the next tree.

"No more vines?" Dylan said hopelessly.

Max shook his head. With no other choice, the boys braced themselves and jumped through the air, reaching for Chance's latest perch and getting slapped in the face by branches along the way.

"Owwww!"

"This isn't as much fun as it looks," panted Max in disappointment, struggling to heave himself on to a limb that looked thick enough to hold his weight.

The monkey watched them, grinning. He deftly leaped to a higher branch.

"Chance," Max wailed, "I was just kidding about the banana punishment!"

"Grab him!" shouted Dylan.

They lunged for the monkey, who promptly jumped to the ground. Chattering triumphantly, Chance leaped across to the bottom of a sheer

rock-face, and proceeded to shin effortlessly to the top with the mask still in his paws. The boys looked on in disbelief.

"I *told* you not to get a monkey," Dylan said through gritted teeth.

Wearily, the boys dropped to the ground. Unable to go straight up the rock-face like Chance, they scrambled up a narrow winding trail in an effort to catch up.

Up on the plateau high above the forest, Dr Prudelock stopped running and caught his breath. He found himself up against the banks of a swift stream flowing through an empty campsite. Gasping for air, he glanced around – and to his delight, saw Chance approaching at speed, still holding on to the mask.

"Ah!" wheezed Prudelock. "Mr Monkey. Hand over the mask and I'm home free . . ."

He started towards Chance, greedily holding out his arms. Then he spotted Max and Dylan in the distance.

"Uh-oh," Prudelock muttered. He glanced around, then ducked out of sight.

Chance ran on towards the stream. Chattering to himself, he glanced over his shoulder as Dylan and Max struggled after him.

"Drop – the – mask," Dylan wheezed.

Dylan was so tired that his words came out as a whisper. Unimpressed, Chance kept right on running.

"I don't – think – he heard you," Max gasped, limping after Dylan.

Dylan pulled in the biggest lungful of air he could manage. "DROP . . . THE . . . MASK!" he roared.

Chance stopped dead in his tracks. He spun round in surprise and looked at Dylan and Max. Then he deliberately dropped the mask into the stream, where it rapidly floated away. Appalled, the boys watched as it swirled and bobbed out of reach.

"Why'd you tell him to drop the mask?" Max yelled. He veered away from the stream, breaking into a sprint as he headed for the campsite toilet block.

Dylan was too tired to ask questions. He simply followed Max and hoped his cousin's actions would make sense some time soon.

Max grabbed a toilet door and, with Dylan's help, tore it off its hinges. The boys staggered away from the open cubicle, completely failing to notice a shocked-looking Dr Prudelock hidden inside, scrunched up on top of the toilet. "Well," Dr Prudelock said feebly to himself as his heart-rate slowed back down to semi-normal. "It smells better with no door . . ."

Max had now uprooted two campsite signs: one with "No Swimming" on it, and the other with a "Dogs on Lead" symbol. He and Dylan dropped the toilet door into the stream and jumped aboard as it spun away from the bank. Using the two signs as paddles, the boys made off after the mask as fast as they could.

"Finally!" Max cheered, spotting Jo, Allie and Timmy about a hundred metres downstream. "Some good news!"

Jo was jumping up and down and shouting something. Paddling harder, Dylan and Max strained to hear what she was saying. Then, with an unpleasant sinking feeling in their stomachs, they did.

"You're heading for a waterfall!" Jo shouted.

"And now back to the bad news," Dylan said feebly.

Chapter Nine

The air up ahead was misty, droplets of water from the waterfall rising like sinister fog. Max and Dylan froze mid-paddle. The mask bobbed merrily on downstream, until it passed the place where Jo, Allie and Timmy were waiting. Without hesitation, Timmy leaped into the foaming water and swam out to the mask. He seized it gently in his teeth and started swimming back.

"Hey!" Dylan yelled as the current swept the raft closer and closer to the lip of the waterfall. "What about us?"

Timmy swam gamely on towards the shore, the white water buffeting him around like a toy. Jo had

to trust that Timmy would make it back without her help. She tore her gaze from her dog and seized Allie's arm, pulling her away to search for some means of rescuing the boys. They ran up and down the bank, hunting for something, anything—

"Follow me!" Jo ordered, catching sight of a branch further downstream which was growing out over the water. She broke into a sprint, adding over her shoulder: "And think heavy thoughts!"

Allie and Jo raced over to the tree Jo had spotted, climbed it and crawled out on the branch, until their weight bent the branch down far enough for the boys to grab hold. They reached out their arms and waited for the raft to approach.

"Aww, the girls are going out on a limb for us," Dylan said. He paused mid-paddle, adding in a pleased kind of voice: "I've got to remember to write that one down . . ."

Jo glanced back over her shoulder. To her relief, Timmy had reached the bank, still holding the mask in his mouth. He clambered out of the water and shook himself dry.

"Gotcha!" shouted Dr Prudelock, pouncing out of the undergrowth beside Timmy.

In a flash, Timmy grabbed the mask again. Barely escaping Prudelock's grasping arms, he jumped straight back into the river.

The boys reached the overhanging branch. They seized it in relief. But before they could draw breath, the branch broke off the tree, plunging all four kids into the fast-flowing water.

"Ahhhh!" shrieked Jo, Allie, Max and Dylan in unison.

"That can't have been your plan," Max gasped, fighting to stay afloat as the others flailed around beside him.

The current raced them onwards. The air was dense with mist, and the waterfall roared ahead of them like a hungry lion. A little way ahead, Max and Dylan's ex-raft bounced up over a wave and disappeared into the fog. Trying not to panic, the cousins clung on to their branch and struggled to escape the current. Every second brought them closer to the precipice.

A whiskery monkey face peeped out of the undergrowth further downstream. Chance chattered brightly and ran to the bank. He seized the end of the broken branch as it sailed up to him,

wedged it between some rocks – and the kids managed to pull themselves to safety!

"All right, Chance!" Max cheered weakly as Allie struggled up the branch and flopped ashore with Dylan and Jo. "That's m'boy!"

"Timmy!" Jo shouted, looking upstream.

Still clinging on to the mask, Timmy was swimming towards the branch. The cousins rushed back out along the broken tree limb, caught Timmy by the scruff of the neck and hauled him out of the water.

"We got you, boy," Jo gasped, burying her face in Timmy's wet neck.

"And I owe you an apology," added Max, shaking his head. "You weren't just jealous of Chance."

A shadow fell across the branch from the shore. The Five turned to see Prudelock watching them, a flash of horrible humour in his eyes.

"Well," Prudelock purred, stooping to tug the tree limb loose, "if I can't have the mask, at least I can have the satisfaction of sending you to your . . ." – he made ironic inverted-comma gestures with his fingers – "*doomy-woomy*."

The villainous vet wrestled harder with the branch. Then behind him, like a wizened little miracle, Chance popped out of the undergrowth. Pulling back his lips, he opened his mouth and screeched. Dr Prudelock leaped out of his skin, lost his balance and tumbled straight into the water.

"Waaaaaaaaaaa . . . !" he howled, and was carried straight over the waterfall.

SPLASSHH!

Gasping and choking out river water, Prudelock struggled to the surface of the pool that sat beneath the waterfall. He had lost his glasses.

A hand snatched him out of the water, then snapped handcuffs on him.

"Like I said . . ." Constable Stubblefield snarled, *"you're nicked."*

Chapter Ten

Back at Jo's house, Ravi's beloved Kranzler-Ross convertible was back, safe and sound. Keen to check it for damage, Ravi had been underneath it for almost an hour.

"Everything down here is spic-and-span," said Ravi happily, his voice floating up from somewhere beneath the old car's chassis. "I was worried about the boot. Winston Churchill once passed out in it."

The cousins high-fived each other proudly.

"What became of your monkey?" George asked Max with interest.

Max grinned. "We gave him to someone he seems to get along with."

There was a familiar screech somewhere across the yard. The little monkey raced into view, wearing a police constable's helmet which was slipping down over his eyes. Puffing slightly, Constable Stubblefield chased after him.

"Chance, get back here!" Constable Stubblefield panted. "Give me back my hat! Give me back my badge!"

"Her uncle runs a monkey sanctuary," Max explained, watching fondly as Chance raced up and over a fence. "Constable Stubblefield's keeping Chance till he can go and live there."

Constable Stubblefield was in danger of wedging herself on the top of the fence as she doggedly pursued the monkey.

"Suppose we should help Constable Stubblefield catch him," Dylan said reluctantly.

"As long as he goes somewhere else after . . ." Jo warned.

The Five raced off after Constable Stubblefield and Chance, whooping encouragement. Whether the encouragement was aimed at the policewoman or the monkey, who could tell?

Epilogue

Allie held a tube of toothpaste in front of Jo's bathroom mirror, smiling brightly at Dylan's videocamera.

"Sticky Situation Number Ninety," Dylan declared. "Foiling a Burglar."

"If you don't have a safe to hide valuables in, here's a cheap and easy way to hide things," Allie chirped, dazzling Dylan's camera lens with her whiter-than-white teeth. "Get an empty toothpaste tube—"

Allie squeezed the tube. The toothpaste slithered out of the end and vanished down the sink.

"Then cut the bottom off it," Allie continued, using a pair of safety scissors to cut the flat end off the tube. "Then you can hide valuables in it – like pearls."

Reaching up around her neck, Allie removed a strand of pearls and dropped it in the open end of the toothpaste tube. She rolled the end of the tube up and replaced it by the sink. "No burglar would ever think to look for something there."

A half-asleep Max stumbled into the bathroom, his pyjamas rumpled and his blond hair standing on end. He fumbled around for a toothbrush, blearily opened the toothpaste tube and squeezed. Allie's pearls shot out of the tube and clattered down the sink.

"What just happened?" Max mumbled in confusion, trying to peer into the spout of the toothpaste tube.

Jo leaned into frame as Allie gave a cry of dismay and scrabbled hopelessly around the plughole. "Next time," she advised the camera with a grin, "we'll show you how to take apart the plumbing under your sink, so you can get your valuables back."

THE CASE OF THE
HOT AIR BA-BOOM!

Read on for Chapter One
of the Famous 5's next
Case File . . .

Hodder
Children's
Books

A division of Hachette Children's Books

Chapter One

A smoky mist was rising off the field in the dim dawn light. Six brightly coloured hot-air balloons stood in a row behind a starting line, waiting for the whistle that would start the Falcongate Three-Day Balloon Race. The only sound was the odd whoosh of gas from the balloons' burners, and the surprised moo of cows in the neighbouring meadow.

Four kids and a dog walked among the balloons, ducking beneath tethering ropes and chatting to one another.

"It's too bad we have to go and see my mum get her botany society award today," Jo said, pushing her dark hair off her face. She glanced longingly at

the balloons. "We could've entered this."

"We could've *won*," Jo's cousin Allie said confidently. "Aunt George has a balloon, and Jo knows how to drive it." She fiddled with the long, colourful silk scarf she was wearing so that it flowed more gracefully around her shoulders. "Or float it," she added with a shrug. "Or whatever you do with it."

"I cook with it," Max said cheerfully. He waved a very long toasting fork at the others, on the end of which was a sausage frazzling nicely over a nearby balloon's propane burner.

"If we can't *enter* the race, maybe we could make some money from it," Dylan said thoughtfully. He took off his glasses and started polishing them vigorously – a sign that he was working out the amount of money he might be able to make. "I'll sell the racers snacks," he added, polishing harder. "Everyone loves snacks."

"Wing Commander Bragg certainly does," Max agreed, gesturing towards a large, military-looking balloon in the middle of the field. "He used to be a tough fighter ace, but he does love his food now."

Ramrod-straight retired RAF officer Wing

Commander Bragg was striding around his balloon basket, studying it from various angles along with his short, stout and entirely dependable wife Gertie. Bragg lifted a police whistle to his lips and gave three sharp blasts.

"Roger, dear," his wife Gertie responded, snapping out a sharp salute as she responded to the whistle blasts. "Fuel secured. Ballast stowed. And a lovely fried-egg sandwich for you . . ." she added.

As Wing Commander Bragg took his sandwich with evident delight, Max broke off a small piece of his own freshly cooked sausage and offered it to Timmy. Ignoring the small piece, Timmy jumped up at the rest of the sausage instead, gobbling the entire smoking chunk straight off the fork.

A nervous-looking starter climbed on to a platform in the middle of the field and started studying his clipboard. The atmosphere sharpened at once. It was clear that the race was about to begin.

"Hey, Allie!" drawled a girl's voice from the basket beneath an enormous balloon monogrammed with the letter 'D'. "What's up with the scarf?"

Daine Dunston and her twin brother Blaine were the rich kids of Falcongate, and liked to make sure

everyone knew it. The Five tried not to have anything to do with them, but the Dunstons were pretty hard to avoid.

"It was a birthday present," Allie said shortly, twisting her scarf around her shoulders again. "It's Italian."

"Oh," smirked Daine Dunston. "I thought a circus clown had lost his trousers."

"Ha, ha, ha!" Allie said, unamused. "You Dunstons – you're very funny. I hope they land in an open sewer," she added to Jo as Daine disappeared back into her basket again in a cloud of mocking laughter.

"Hey, Blaine, Daine," Jo shouted up at the monogrammed balloon. "What's the 'D' on your balloon stand for? 'Duh'?"

"Hee, hee – zing!" Allie chuckled, her good humour firmly back in place.

The starter raised his starting pistol. "Balloonists," he said in rather a weedy voice, "let the Falcongate Three-Day Race begin!" He fiddled with the pistol, wincing and muttering: "Oh, I hate this part . . ." before plugging his ears and firing the pistol into the air.

POP!

One of the balloons exploded into shreds of brightly coloured silk. A second rapidly deflated, lurching wildly through the air with its pilot hanging on to the ropes for dear life. A third balloon snapped all its connecting ropes, leaving a puzzled pilot sitting on the ground in his gondola basket as the balloon part of his equipment sailed into the brightening sky. The Five watched with concern as Wing Commander Bragg's balloon jerked and began to rise extremely slowly.

"I know, honeypot!" shouted Gertie as Bragg blew his whistle frantically. "The regulator's been sabotaged! We're not getting enough lift."

The Braggs' balloon drifted lazily into the highest branches of a tall tree, its basket snagging on the branches. A string of powerlines hung dangerously close.

"They'll be OK," Jo said, peering anxiously up into the tree. "As long as the wind doesn't push them toward the power lines."

A gust of wind riffled Allie's scarf. The Braggs' gondola basket started to swing towards the power lines.

"Oh, me and my big mouth," Jo muttered, breaking into a sprint with the others close behind.

Read the adventures of George and the
original Famous Five in

THE
FAMOUS FIVE'S
SURVIVAL GUIDE

Packed with useful information on surviving outdoors and solving mysteries, here is the one mystery that the Famous Five never managed to solve. See if you can follow the trail to discover the location of the priceless Royal Dragon of Siam.

The perfect book for all fans of mystery, adventure and the Famous Five

ISBN 9780340970836